Who is he?

Besides being best friends and doing practically everything together, the four of us run a birthday-party entertainment service for little kids. So Stephanie's news wasn't good news.

"The Duvas party tomorrow afternoon," Stephanie said. "We've been canceled!"

"Canceled?!" I said. "Why?"

"Freddie decided he didn't want us," she mumbled.

"Didn't want us?" Kate squawked. "I don't believe it! What a little twerp."

"So who *does* Freddie want?" Patti asked.

"I was getting to that," Stephanie said. "Some guy named Mandrake the Magician."

"Who is he?" Kate said.

"Nobody seems to know," Stephanie replied. "He's very mysterious. He even wears a mask. But Freddie saw Mandrake at a party and apparently that's all he's talked about ever since. He keeps going on about how Mandrake can make coins vanish into thin air and pull Coke cans out of folded newspapers, that kind of stuff."

"This is very serious," Patti said. "Little kids *love* magic. We could totally lose our audience!"

Look for these and other books
in the Sleepover Friends Series:

Stephanie and the Magician

Susan Saunders

AN
APPLE
PAPERBACK

SCHOLASTIC INC.
New York Toronto London Auckland Sydney

ISBN 0-590-42814-4

12 11 10 9 8 7 6 5 4 3 2 1   9/8 0 1 2 3 4/9

Printed in the U.S.A.   28

First Scholastic printing, November 1989

Chapter
1

"There's the joke that goes, 'What's the difference between a peanut-butter-and-jelly sandwich and an elephant?' " Patti Jenkins raised her voice to a high-pitched squeak.

"An . . . elephant . . . doesn't . . . stick to the roof of your mouth!" I growled back in a raspy voice — I'm Lauren Hunter —. Then I added a couple of "Woofs!"

Kate Beekman sighed and shook her head. "No good. We've done that one too many times already." She leaned back against the headboard of her bed and scrunched up her forehead. Then she smiled. "I've got it! How about, 'On which side does an ostrich have the most feathers?' " And she answered

1

herself, "On the outside, of course!"

I groaned. "That joke's too corny to live!"

"Besides," Patti said, "ostriches don't have much to do with circuses. That's the theme of the party, isn't it?"

"Yep. Freddie Duva loves circuses. Mrs. Duva told Stephanie's mom she's even going to have a cake in the shape of a circus tent, and give out wooden circus animals as favors," Kate said. "Plus all of the kids are supposed to dress up in circus costumes."

It was a Friday night. Kate, Patti, and I were upstairs in Kate's bedroom. We were running through our party routines while we waited for Stephanie Green to show up for our weekly sleepover.

Besides being best friends and doing practically everything together, the four of us run a birthday-party entertainment service for little kids. Patti dresses up as a sort of combination space alien and tooth fairy. She calls herself Sparkly and the name fits. She wears antennas on her head made out of a plastic headband, pipe cleaners, and Styrofoam balls. She paints stars and comets all over her face with glittery silver eyeshadow and those bright-colored zinc-oxide sunblocks. She also wears a multicolored tie-dyed T-shirt and blue glitter tights. She even talks in a high sparkly voice.

As for me, I'm Barkly, the Party Dog. I dress up in my mom's old fake-fur jacket, brown tights, and fuzzy brown mittens for paws. Then I paint brown, black, and yellow spots on my face, and tie my hair into dog ears. Oh, and I say "Woof! Woof!" a lot.

Sounds dumb, right? But the kids seem to love it. Patti and I blow up balloons, jump around, tell hokey jokes, and all these five- and six- and seven-year-olds go crazy! Kate and Stephanie record the whole thing for the parents with a video camera that we'll probably be paying off for years.

Still, I have to admit, I kind of enjoy the whole thing. Who doesn't like being a star, even if it's just for an hour or two at a little kids' party?

A horn beeped twice out in front of the Beekmans' house. Kate pushed open her bedroom window. "Stephanie's here!" she announced. Now our weekly sleepover could officially begin.

Stephanie rang the front door bell, and Mrs. Beekman let her in. Then we heard her come clumping up the stairs, instead of bouncing up, the way she usually does.

"She doesn't sound too happy," Patti murmured. Kate and I nodded.

After eleven years of having her parents all to herself, Stephanie's no longer the only child in the Green family. In fact, as of a couple of weeks ago, she's only one out of *three* — Mrs. Green had twins! It would be quite an adjustment for anyone, and Stephanie had been getting mopier and mopier.

"How are things at your house?" Kate asked when Stephanie pushed open the bedroom door.

"Just great," Stephanie replied glumly. She made a face. "Except for the fact that my parents seem to have forgotten that I'm alive. The only time they ever talk to me anymore is to tell me to quiet down." She dropped her red canvas tote on the floor and flopped onto the bed next to Kate.

"The twins have only been home for ten days," Patti said soothingly. "Things will settle down soon."

"I'm not so sure," Stephanie muttered. "That might be true with *one* baby brother or sister, but I don't stand a chance now that there's one of *each*! I'm beginning to feel like the Invisible Girl."

That didn't sound like Stephanie at all. She's so

positive about everything. Also, she's always been the apple of her parents' eyes.

"What do you mean, exactly?" Kate asked her.

Stephanie couldn't have looked more miserable. "Let's just say that if my dad hadn't been on his way to Romanos" — Romanos is a store at the mall that sells everything — "to pick up more baby formula, I probably would have had to trudge through the snow all the way to your house," she mumbled. "He can't bear to tear himself away from the *twins* for a minute!" Stephanie looked like she was about to cry. "I have to face it: Twins are special, and I guess there's nothing very special about me."

Kate and Patti and I exchanged worried looks. We'd never heard Stephanie say anything like that before. She always had so much confidence in herself.

"There's plenty that's special about you!" I exclaimed.

Stephanie frowned doubtfully at me. "Like what?"

"Well, you know all about fashion," I said. Stephanie's the only fifth-grader I know who already has her own style of dressing, like *always* wearing red, black, and white.

But Stephanie just sniffed. "Big deal!" she replied. "That's just a fancy way of saying I like to shop!"

"You're a great dancer!" Patti put in quickly. It's true, Stephanie knows the steps to all the latest dances.

"So are ten million other kids who watch Video Trax," Stephanie answered gloomily.

"Would *we* want you for a friend if you weren't special?" Kate said with a smile. She was trying to lighten up Stephanie's mood a little.

"Yeah, Stephanie. Where would we be without you?" I said. I usually hate saying corny things like that, but this time I really meant it.

Even though I've only known Stephanie for a year and a half, I couldn't imagine life without her. Just three Sleepover Friends? No way!

Of course, when we started out, there were only two of us: Kate and me. We've lived on Pine Street, just one house apart, since we were born. We started playing together when we were toddlers. By kindergarten, we were old friends. That's when the sleepovers began.

Every Friday night, either I would sleep over at Kate's house, or she'd sleep over at mine. It soon became such a regular thing that Kate's dad nicknamed us the Sleepover Twins.

Not that Kate and I are very much alike. She's small and blonde; I'm tall with dark-brown hair. She's always sensible; I tend to let my imagination run away with me. Still, as different as Kate and I are, we've always gotten along.

At our sleepovers, we graduated from playing dress-up in our moms' clothes and melting s'mores all over the toaster oven, to Video Trax, Mad Libs, and my special onion dip on barbecue potato chips. And through it all, we never had a major argument.

Then Stephanie moved from the city to a house at the other end of Pine Street. We got to know each other because we were both in 4A, Mr. Civello's class.

I thought Stephanie was great. She had lots of wild ideas and was always coming up with fun things to do. I wanted Kate to get to know her, too, so I invited Stephanie to a Friday sleepover at my house. . . .

Talk about a total bummer! Kate thought Stephanie was an airhead who was only interested in clothes. Stephanie thought Kate took herself *much* too seriously.

My brother, Roger — he's a junior in high school — said the problem was obvious: "They may *seem* different, but when push comes to shove" — which it practically had — "they're too much alike. Both bossy!"

Now, I can be pretty stubborn myself. I decided I wasn't going to give up on Kate and Stephanie becoming friends. I was just going to have to kind of ease them into it. . . .

The next Friday, Stephanie asked me — and Kate, because I insisted — to sleep over at her house. Mrs. Green made her delicious peanut-butter-chocolate-chip cookies. Kate thawed out a little. The only thing she likes as much as chocolate is peanut butter. Then we watched three movies on Cinema Classics. That definitely softened Kate up. She's a real movie freak.

Then Kate asked Stephanie to a Friday night at her house. And little by little, the Sleepover Twins became the Sleepover Friends.

Not that Kate and Stephanie automatically saw eye to eye. They still had plenty of disagreements.

Which is just one of the reasons I was glad when Patti Jenkins showed up this year in the same fifth-grade class as Kate, Stephanie, and me.

Patti's from the city, too. She and Stephanie even went to the same school for a couple of years. But you'd never guess it to talk to her. Patti's as shy as Stephanie is outgoing. Patti's also kind, thoughtful, and one of the smartest kids at Riverhurst Elementary.

Stephanie wanted Patti to be part of our gang. Kate and I agreed. We both liked Patti right away. So fifth grade had barely gotten off the ground, before there were *four* Sleepover Friends!

What are we friends for, if not to cheer each other up when one of us is down? And Stephanie was definitely down.

I remembered a joke I'd heard on TV: " 'Parents spend the first part of a kid's life getting her to walk and talk, and the rest of it getting her to sit still and shut up.' Cheer up, Stephanie! It'll be the twins' turn to be invisible in six years or so."

"Your jokes are getting worse and worse, Lauren," Stephanie said, but at least she smiled. Then she smacked her forehead with her hand. "Wow — I almost forgot!"

"What?" the rest of us said.

"The Duvas' party tomorrow afternoon," Stephanie cried. "We've been canceled!"

"Canceled?!" I said. "Why?"

"Does Freddie have chicken pox?" Patti asked. "Half the kids in Horace's class have it." Patti's little brother Horace is in the first grade.

Stephanie looked uneasy. "No — Freddie's not sick." She bit her lip. "The Duvas *are* having the party. Freddie just decided he didn't want Sparkly and Barkly," she mumbled.

"Didn't want us!" Kate squawked. "I don't believe it! What a little twerp!"

"Mrs. Duva was very apologetic," Stephanie said. "Since she canceled us so late, she's going to pay us half our fee, anyway. We'll get fifteen dollars for doing nothing."

"Who cares about the fee?! That spoiled brat!" Kate was outraged. I was pretty steamed up, myself. That Freddie Duva had some nerve, especially for a seven-year-old!

"So who *does* Freddie want?" Patti asked.

"I was getting to that," Stephanie said. "Some guy named Mandrake the Magician."

"I've never heard of him," Kate said. "Who is he?"

"Nobody seems to know," Stephanie replied. "He's very mysterious. He even wears a mask!"

"Nobody seems to know?" I repeated. "Then how do they get in touch with him?"

"He can't just appear by magic!" Kate said with a snort.

"No. He has an ad, with a telephone number, in the *Riverhurst Clarion*," Stephanie said — she'd done some research into this Mandrake character. "Freddie Duva saw Mandrake at Brucie Rodwin's party, and apparently that's all he's talked about ever since. Mrs. Duva said he keeps going on about how Mandrake can make coins vanish into thin air and pull Coke cans out of folded newspapers, that kind of stuff." Stephanie shrugged. "I guess this Mandrake has a pretty good act."

"This is serious," Patti said. "Very serious. Little kids *love* magic. We could totally lose our audience!"

Chapter
2

For a moment we all just stared at each other. Stephanie wasn't the only one who was feeling down now.

"Sparkly and Barkly, down the tubes!" I exclaimed. I didn't even want to think about it.

"And no more money to pay back Mr. Green!" Kate groaned. Stephanie's dad bought the video camera for us, and we're paying him off a little at a time with the money we make from the parties.

"There must be something we can do," I said.

"First of all, we'll have to come up with a bunch of funnier jokes," Stephanie said.

"We'd better do a lot more than that," Kate said. "Maybe we should advertise in the newspaper, like

Mandrake. And beef up our act with new stuff kids really like.''

"Like what?" I asked.

"How about story-telling?" Patti suggested.

"Not exciting enough," Kate said. "They can get that at the library."

Stephanie snapped her fingers. "I know! I went to a party in the city once, where they had four trained dogs that turned flips, and — "

"The only dog we've got among the four of us is Bullwinkle," I broke in. "And I don't see him turning flips." Bullwinkle is actually my brother's dog. He's an out-of-control, 130-pound, mostly Newfoundland giant. I mean, the dog is *untrainable*.

"We want to entertain the kids, not cream them," Kate added. Bullwinkle has a way of knocking people flat and standing on them to lick their faces. "It just wouldn't work."

"We do have four kittens, though," Stephanie pointed out.

"Do you really think they're ready to star in a show?" Kate asked, with a pointed glance at her calico kitten, Fredericka. Fredericka was in her favorite position — curled up in a tight, little ball, fast asleep.

"Maybe you're right," Stephanie admitted. "Let's see. . . . Mimes do parties!" She didn't sound very enthusiastic.

"Ugh! I can't stand mimes," Patti said with a shiver. "The way they get right up in your face gives me the creeps."

"Anyway, it takes years of training to be a mime," I said. I actually like them, but I figured our chances of teaching Bullwinkle to do a triple back flip were better than our chances of pulling off a mime act. "What about a puppet show?"

"That's not a bad idea," Kate agreed. "Hey — I think we've even got some puppets somewhere. My uncle sent them to us on his trip to Indonesia a few years ago."

"Let's check them out!" Stephanie said.

"They're pretty fierce-looking," Kate warned. "They've all got knives and spears and swords with really convincing blood spots on them. My mom wouldn't hang them up anywhere. She stuck them in the basement."

"The fiercer they are, the better little kids will like them," Patti said. "Horace is always pretending he's a Ninja warrior who can kill his enemies with a single blow — he loves that kind of stuff.''

"I hope Jeremy is not going to be like that!'' Stephanie said, wrinkling her nose. Jeremy is the boy twin at the Greens'. The girl is named Emma.

"Not for a couple of years yet,'' Kate said with a grin. "Come on. Let's take a look at those puppets.''

As we headed down to the basement, Stephanie asked, "Where's Melissa?'' Melissa is Kate's little sister, better known as Melissa the Monster. She's constantly spying on us, so it's only smart to keep her whereabouts in mind.

"Watching TV in the living room with Mom and Dad,'' Kate said. "We're safe for a while, at least.''

"Anything to eat?'' I asked casually as we crossed the kitchen to the basement door. After all, it *had* been a couple of hours since dinner.

"Lauren, have we ever had a sleepover with nothing to eat?'' Kate asked. She looked at her watch. "Must be a record,'' she said to the others. "Lauren's gone for twenty-five whole minutes without mentioning food once.''

Kate and Stephanie call me the Bottomless Pit, or the Endless Stomach. But I think of myself as just having a healthy appetite.

15

"Why don't we look at the puppets first?" Patti said in her most businesslike voice. "Then we can have snacks."

"Okay," I said. But I couldn't help staring at the Beekmans' refrigerator longingly before following the others down the basement stairs. I've probably spent more time rummaging through that refrigerator than Kate has!

My basement is a total disaster area, but the Beekmans' basement is as tidy as the rest of their house. It's amazing. They've got these labeled boxes stacked neatly against the walls, and the shelves are all perfectly arranged. Even the floor is so clean you could eat off of it. Ooops! I was thinking about food again.

"The puppets should be in here," Kate said, walking over to a blue cabinet in the corner.

She unlatched the cabinet doors, and there they were: three large puppets with big wooden heads. The two men puppets wore silk shirts and flared silk pants. One was dressed in light blue. He had a gold crown on his head, and his thin mustache curled up at the ends like a smile.

The other was dressed all in black, with a red sash. He had a pointy beard and dangling glass ear-

16

rings in his ears. He also had a mean expression on his face.

Both men were carrying swords with red dots painted on them to look like blood. The man in black held a spear, too.

"I can guess what the story is here," Stephanie said. "These two guys must be fighting over her." She pointed to the third puppet, a beautiful lady.

She was wearing a shimmery green gown and smiling. But this was definitely a bloodthirsty bunch, because she was also holding a great, big knife!

"But they're the kind with strings," Patti said. She sounded doubtful. "They're a lot more complicated to operate than hand puppets."

Fine gray strings were attached on one end to the puppets' heads, arms, hands, knees, and feet. On the other end they were attached to six wooden X's — two for each puppet.

"How hard can it be?" Stephanie said, reaching for the puppet with the gold crown.

We had our answer pretty quickly — really hard! Before Stephanie had even gotten the puppet out of the cabinet, his strings were all twisted up. It took us ages to untangle them. And Stephanie still couldn't get the puppet to work.

"I can't do anything right!" she cried. "Every time I try to make him swing his sword around, he stabs himself in the side."

She set him down, shaking her head.

"Let's see . . . ," Kate said, lifting out the bad guy.

But she didn't do any better. His spear got hooked in his strings. When she tried to unhook it by moving the wooden X's around, the puppet waved his arms and legs wildly and jerked his head up and down like a turtle.

Stephanie, Patti, and I burst out laughing. "He looks like Robert Ellwanger!" Patti said through her giggles. Robert Ellwanger's in 5C. He's known as the biggest geek at Riverhurst Elementary.

Kate sighed. "The puppet's supposed to look tough, not like a dork!"

We tried out the lady puppet, too. But no matter how we moved the X's around, all three puppets looked jerky and uncoordinated. They didn't look fierce or dangerous at all.

"Somehow, I don't think puppets are the answer," Kate said at last, "unless one of us is an undercover Pinocchio." She stuck the puppet in black back into the cabinet. "I've had it. Let's go get something to eat."

As usual, the Beekmans' fridge was crammed with great leftovers. Both of Kate's parents are terrific cooks. If I were Kate, I don't think I'd ever do anything but eat. "Here's some pineapple chicken," Kate said, handing me a plate covered with foil. "There's also cold spaghetti and meatballs, garlic bread, fruit salad. . . ." She rattled off a whole mouth-watering list of possibilities. ". . . and my super-fudge, and Lauren's special dip, of course." Over the years, I've perfected an onion-soup-olives-bacon-bits-and-sour-cream dip that's dynamite with barbecue potato chips.

We started transferring food from the fridge to two big trays. We never eat in the Beekmans' kitchen when Melissa's around. Instead, we always load everything on trays and lug it all up to Kate's bedroom, for privacy.

Patti was taking some plates out of the cupboard to add to the pile when she noticed a copy of the *Clarion* on the counter. "Hey, here's the paper," she said, opening it up. "Let's look for Mandrake's ad."

Patti found it in the classifieds, under *Entertain-*

ment. " 'Why is everyone talking about the Magnificent Mandrake. . . ,' " she read out loud.

"Magnificent Mandrake!" Kate muttered.

"Everybody's talking about him? I never even heard of him until about forty minutes ago!" I added.

" '. . . Magnificent Mandrake the Magician?' " Patti read on. " 'Invite him to *your* party, and find out! Call four-two-seven-oh-eight-three-seven.' "

Kate put down the king-size bottle of Dr Pepper she was holding, and reached for the wall phone. "Let's just see what the Magnificent Mandrake has to say for himself!" she said. "Four-two-seven-oh-eight-three-seven. . . ." Kate held the phone out so Patti and Stephanie and I could listen in, too.

"Kate! What if he. . . ," Patti protested nervously.

"We're going to get to the bottom of this!" Kate said in a firm voice. There's no stopping Kate when she's set on something.

The phone rang once, twice. . . . Then it was picked up.

Over a background of weird, spooky music, a deep, hollow voice announced, "You've reached the residence of Magnificent Mandrake the Magician.

I'm busy performing incredible magical feats right now, so I'm unable to come to the phone. But if you will leave your name and number, I'll be sure to get back to you. . . ."

Kate hung up the phone, with a disgusted look. "If you ask me, an answering machine is *not* very magical."

"And we don't know any more about him now than we did before," Patti said, disappointed.

Stephanie had been peering at the *Clarion* over Patti's shoulder. " 'Roast-a-grams. Balloon bouquets,' " she murmured. She was still checking out the *Entertainment* listings. " 'Palmist. Juggler. . . .' Hey," she said. "I used to be able to juggle a little."

She put the newspaper down, and grabbed three small plates out of the cupboard. Then she started flinging them into the air!

"Be careful!" Patti warned. "They'll break!"

"Don't worry! They're plastic. . . ," Stephanie said. She was concentrating so hard on her juggling that the tip of her tongue was sticking out between her teeth.

"Two of them are. The third one's — " Kate began.

That's when Melissa stuck her head into the kitchen and shrieked, "I'm telling Mom you guys are throwing dishes around!"

Stephanie only took her eyes off the plates for a second, but it was enough to break her rhythm. She managed to catch two of the plates but the third one — it just had to be the pottery plate, right? — hit the floor and shattered into about fifty pieces.

"Oh, wow!" Stephanie cried, scrambling to pick the pieces up. "I'm sorry, Kate!"

"I don't think juggling is the answer." Kate squatted down to help Stephanie. She glared at Melissa, who was still standing in the doorway. "But maybe we could hire Mandrake the Magnificent to make Melissa disappear," she growled.

"And maybe I could hire him to turn you into a frog!" Melissa shouted back. She crossed her eyes at her older sister and pulled the corners of her mouth down with her fingers.

Melissa's sort of a funny-looking kid to begin with. She's got straggly brown hair, pale blue eyes, and a pointy nose, and the face she was making didn't help her looks any. She marched over to the refrigerator and yanked open the door. "Mandrake's good," she said, peering inside. "But I guess he's not that good."

"You've actually seen Mandrake?" I asked.

"Sure — at Debbie Waxman's party, last week." Debbie Waxman is a third-grader, like Melissa.

"I didn't know that!" Kate exclaimed.

"You don't know much." Melissa flipped open a can of ginger ale. "My friends and I are way too old to watch a couple of dumb clowns hopping around," she added disdainfully. She took a swig of her soda.

"Well, excu-u-use me!" I said, speaking for *one* of the dumb clowns. Melissa was really getting too big for her eight-year-old britches!

"Magnificent Mandrake was at Martin Yates's party, too," Melissa added.

"Martin Yates is a *fourth-grader*," Stephanie said. She dumped the pieces of broken plate into the trash can.

"So Mandrake is going for older kids, as well," Patti said. She narrowed her eyes thoughtfully. "Melissa, what does Mandrake look like?" she asked.

Melissa frowned importantly. "Well. . . ." She

23

concentrated, trying to remember. "He dresses in black. He wears a big black hat, a black sweater, black pants — oh — and a black mask!"

Stephanie nodded. "How tall is he?" she asked. "And what color is his hair?"

"He's got dark hair," Melissa said. "And he's about as tall as Lauren."

"What?" the four of us yelped at the same time.

I'm practically the tallest girl in fifth-grade (Patti's a little taller), but I'm only ten and a half. That meant Mandrake was either an adult midget, or . . .

Chapter
3

"Do you mean to tell me Mandrake is a *kid*?" Kate cried, staring at her little sister. "Think carefully before you answer, Melissa."

"Of course he is!" Melissa sniffed, as though we were hopelessly dense.

"Which kid?" I asked her.

"Who can tell, with the hat and the mask and everything?" Melissa said, shrugging her shoulders. "I don't have X-ray eyes, you know." She turned and headed back to the living room.

"Who could Mandrake be?" Stephanie said when Melissa had gone. "If he's not any taller than that, he's probably not even in junior high. He's in elementary school like us!"

"Elementary school. . . ?" Patti looked thoughtful. "What about Henry Larkin, or Larry Jackson?" she suggested. "They did magic tricks at the school talent show."

"I know. But they weren't any good," Stephanie put in. "Anyway, Larry Jackson has reddish hair, and his ears stick out. He'd be easy to recognize."

"And Henry Larkin's almost as short as Stephanie and Kate," I added. "Besides, Henry wouldn't be so sneaky about trying to put us out of business. He'd probably go into business *with* us!"

Henry's in Mrs. Mead's class like the four of us, and he's a good guy. I was sure he wouldn't go skulking around behind a black mask.

Kate picked up one tray and Patti picked up the other. We headed up the stairs toward Kate's bedroom.

"There are probably thirty boys in fifth grade alone who are Lauren's height," Patti said after Kate had closed the door behind us. "Not to mention all the tall fourth-graders, and short sixth-graders around."

"If we really want to find out who Mandrake is, there's only one way to do it," Stephanie said. "We've got to get a look at him in action!"

26

"How are we going to manage that?" I asked. "We can't crash Freddie Duva's party." I giggled at the thought of it!

"But that's exactly what we're going to do," Stephanie said, with a big grin.

I stared at her. "You've got to be kidding," I said.

"Don't you think somebody would notice four uninvited *fifth*-graders at a second-grader's party?" Kate asked, raising a blonde eyebrow.

"Who said anything about *four* crashers? One of us will go in. Meanwhile the rest of us will hide in the bushes outside, in case Mandrake beats a retreat!" Stephanie was sounding more like her normal, wheeling-and-dealing self every minute. It did her good to get away from the babies.

"Oh, yeah?" Kate didn't sound convinced. She and Patti set the trays down on the rug and opened a bottle of Dr Pepper and a bag of chips. "Which of us is going to go in?"

Stephanie pulled the foil off the pineapple chicken, and picked up a drumstick. "It has to be you, Kate," she answered. "You're the shortest."

"No way!" Kate yelped. "You're as short as I am!"

"Uh-uh. The last time Mrs. Cooperman measured us in gym, I was at least half an inch taller, almost three-quarters!" Stephanie said, taking a bite of her chicken.

It was true. Stephanie has been growing lately, maybe in self-defense because of the twins.

"I won't do it!" Kate said, with a scowl. "I'll stick out like a sore thumb. I'll be at least a head taller than everybody else!"

"Don't worry," Stephanie said soothingly. "It's a circus *costume* party, remember? We'll dress you up so that no one will be able to tell how tall you are."

"Sure," Kate growled.

"Come on, Kate. We have to know what the competition is like, don't we?" I sat on the floor next to the trays and snared a piece of chicken. "Besides, I'm sure if you see Mandrake in person, you'll be able to figure out who he is!"

"Please?" Patti put in.

"Oh, all right!" Kate said. "But you guys better make sure I'm *totally* disguised. If anybody at school ever hears I crashed a second-grade party, I'll never live it down!"

"You'll be disguised, all right," Stephanie promised. "I've just thought of the perfect costume for you — an elephant!"

"An elephant?" Kate glared at Stephanie. "I beg your pardon!" It was clear she wasn't crazy about the idea.

"It'll be great," Stephanie went on, ignoring the look on Kate's face. "You can wear your gray tights, and my dad has an old gray sweater that'll absolutely swallow you. We can pad it out, too. Then we'll make a huge elephant head for you out of gray construction paper. . . ."

"It does sound like the perfect disguise," Patti giggled.

"My dad was just replacing the vent on our clothes dryer," I said. "There's some of that hose stuff left over. I'll bet it would make a terrific elephant's trunk."

"And you can walk kind of stooped, Kate, because your arms will be the elephant's front legs," Stephanie added. "Then no one will be able to tell you're taller than everybody else."

"Whoop-tee-do," Kate said crossly.

"Since the Duvas live closest to me," Stephanie went on, scooping up some dip with a potato chip, "and the party starts at two, we should meet at my house around a quarter to one. That should give us plenty of time to cut out the elephant head, get Kate dressed, and get over to the Duvas'. Animals are your specialty, Patti, so you can be responsible for the head. . . ."

Patti does love animals — she's thinking about being a vet some day. But she shook her head. "I can't," she said. "I've got to be at the university science library from eleven to one to work on a Quarks project." The Quarks is a club in Riverhurst for kids who are really good at science.

"Oh, well, the three of us will make the head, then," Stephanie said.

"I'll wear it, but I won't make it," Kate said firmly. "I'm rotten at art."

Stephanie turned to me. "It looks like it's up to us, Lauren," she said.

I nodded reluctantly. I'm not much good at art either, but I didn't want to let the Sparkly and Barkly Party Service down.

"We'll get Kate dressed," Stephanie continued. "And as soon as Patti comes, we'll sneak through a few backyards to the Duvas'. Then, while Kate goes inside, the rest of us will hide nearby. We'll be responsible for seeing what Mandrake does when he leaves the party. Check?"

"Check!" Patti said.

"Check!" I agreed.

"Aye-aye, chief," Kate muttered.

"Well, that takes care of Mandrake," I said. "Now how about coming up with some new ideas for the Sparkly and Barkly Show?"

"I have one," Patti said. "While I'm at the library, I'll look up palmistry — palm reading. It was one of the things listed under 'Entertainment' in the *Clarion*."

"At the science library?" Kate said. "Palm reading isn't exactly scientific."

"No, but there's a whole section on things like ESP, reincarnation, and UFOs," Patti said. "I'm sure there'll be something about palm reading." She looked down at her own palm. "All these little lines are supposed to mean something." She grinned. "I'll practice on myself first, and then I'll try it out on you guys."

"Great!" Stephanie said. "Maybe I'll work on improving my juggling. . . ."

"I don't think there are enough plates in Riverhurst," Kate said. "But I might fiddle with the puppets a little more. . . ."

"In the meantime," I broke in, "why don't we look at Kate's copy of last year's *Roundup*? It may give us some clues about Magnificent Mandrake."

The Riverhurst Elementary School *Roundup* is a little booklet that comes out at the end of every school year. In it there are pictures of Mrs. Wainwright, the principal of Riverhurst Elementary, all of the teachers, and every single class, first grade through sixth.

"That's a great idea!" Kate said. "We can write down all the possible Mandrakes, and eliminate the impossibles."

So while we munched our way through chicken, dip, super-fudge, and samples of most of the other food in the Beekmans' refrigerator, we looked at pictures of boys.

First we checked out our grade.

"So we're sure it's not Larry or Henry?" Stephanie asked, pointing to their grinning faces.

"Yes. And Michael Pastore is too short," Kate put in. Michael's a boy in 5A that Stephanie used to like.

"What about Todd Farrell?" Stephanie suggested. "He's tall enough."

32

"No way. He's much too shy," I said. "Todd would *never* be able to stand up in front of a crowd like that, much less do anything entertaining once he was there." I flipped the page. "What about Alan Reese?"

"If Alan were Mandrake, his little brothers would have spilled the beans long ago," Kate said. "They're both total blabbermouths."

"Wayne Miller and Ronny Wallace are too gross," I said.

"You're right," Patti nodded. "Wayne can't go for more than three minutes without burping, or making some other horrible noise."

"And Ronny can't make a move without Wayne," Kate said.

"Kyle's too short, too," Stephanie said.

"Besides, he'd never give up his Saturday afternoons," Kate said quickly. Kyle Hubbard is even more of a film freak than Kate is, and he always spends his Saturdays at the latest sci-fi flicks in town.

Stephanie turned the page and started to giggle. "Look at Robert Ellwanger," she said, lifting the book so we could all see. "Some boys have gotten a lot cuter since last year, but not Robert. This could have been taken yesterday!"

33

In the picture, Robert Ellwanger was sitting up very straight in his chair. The photographer's flash was shining off his teeth. His pants were too short. Even his sneakers were wrong.

"Once a geek, always a geek," Kate said, shaking her head.

"I feel kind of sorry for him," Patti said softly. Patti is always saying things like that. She was just born nice.

"It's too bad boys can't have makeovers, like the ones in *Teen* magazine," I commented.

"Yeah. The first thing to go would be that haircut," Stephanie said. Stephanie doesn't believe in being *too* nice. She was right about Robert's hair, though. It's parted way over on the side, and always looks as though he ironed it flat. "His hair could have been borrowed from a kid on one of those fifties sitcoms!"

"What gets me is, he thinks he's kind of cool," Kate said. "In this picture, he's actually giving Jenny Carlin the eye!"

"He really is!" I said, staring at the picture.

Robert's eyes were sliding over to the left, permanently glued to Jenny Carlin in her pink jumpsuit.

"Check out the way she's smirking at the camera," said Kate.

"Yuck!" Stephanie said.

"Ick!" Patti and I agreed.

Don't worry — Jenny Carlin can't stand us, either. And she especially can't stand me. At the beginning of this year she decided she liked a boy in our class named Pete Stone. But around the same time, Pete Stone started liking *me*. It certainly wasn't because of anything *I'd* done. He only liked me for about two weeks, anyway.

But since Jenny thinks everybody's as boy-crazy as she is, she was sure I had done something to make Pete interested. Believe it or not, she's *never* forgiven me for it. Now she tries to get in digs at me whenever she can.

"Could you believe her act in the cafeteria today at lunch?" Kate asked.

"She was so loud, they probably heard her in Dannerville," I said. Dannerville's about ten miles away from Riverhurst.

" 'Oh, Pete,' " Stephanie gushed. " 'I had no *idea* you were such a good basketball player, until I saw you in the park yesterday afternoon. . . .' " We all burst out laughing. Stephanie can do a great imitation of Jenny's screechy voice.

"It was mostly for our benefit, too. She knew we were only sitting three tables away," Patti said. "Poor Pete looked really embarrassed."

"I wonder how Angela can stand her," Stephanie said. Angela is Jenny's faithful sidekick.

"Well. . . . Robert Ellwanger seems to like her fine," I said, tapping the picture in the *Roundup*.

Stephanie suddenly grinned. "Maybe we should make their day," she said.

"Whose day?" I asked.

"Robert's and Jenny's! Let's get the phone in here," Stephanie said. The Beekmans' upstairs phone sits out in the hall, but fortunately it has a *very* long cord.

Kate held her finger up to her lips, noiselessly opened her bedroom door, and tiptoed out into the hall. She was back in a flash with the phone. She handed it to Stephanie.

We have a long history of phoning Robert Ellwanger — calling him up has been the "dare" part of more than one Truth or Dare game.

It's easy to get Robert's number. There's only *one* Ellwanger family in Riverhurst.

"Four-seven-two-oh-one-six-five," Stephanie repeated after the operator. She clicked off and quickly dialed the number.

The phone rang a few times. Then Robert answered it himself.

"Hello?" he said. His voice sounded high and squeaky as usual.

Kate, Patti, and I covered our mouths with our hands so we wouldn't burst into giggles.

"Hellooo, Robert," Stephanie said in her screechy, Jenny Carlin voice.

"Who's this?" Robert said, lowering his voice about an octave.

"Jenny, silly," Stephanie cooed. She rolled her eyes at us.

"Jenny Carlin?" Robert squeaked again in his excitement.

"That's right," Jenny/Stephanie said. "I was wondering if you'd like to come to my house tomorrow afternoon around two-thirty. I'm having some kids over and — "

"Oh, wow! I can't!" Robert said. He sounded like it was the disappointment of a lifetime. "I'm really sorry, Jenny, but I have an appointment tomorrow afternoon. Uh — maybe another time?"

"Definitely," Stephanie screeched. "We absolutely have to get together soon. Bye-eee, Robert."

"Good-bye. Soon," Robert added before he hung up the phone.

Stephanie hung up, too.

The four of us looked at each other and cracked up.

"Robert Ellwanger turned Jenny Carlin down!" Stephanie and I exclaimed at the same time. "Unbelievable!"

"I don't know about making Robert's day," Kate said, "but he certainly made mine!"

Chapter
4

The sleepover at Kate's definitely cheered Stephanie up. But by the time Kate and I got to the Greens' on Saturday afternoon, she was totally bummed out again.

Stephanie answered the door herself, one second after we'd rung the bell. "Sssh," she said in a low voice. "Don't take your coats off." Her face looked as if it had settled into a permanent frown. "We're going to the apartment. All the stuff we'll need for Kate's costume is out there already."

When the new wing for the babies was added onto the main house, Mr. Green also had his contractor build a little house in the backyard. He told Stephanie it was going to be a home office for him.

39

But on Stephanie's birthday her parents gave her the key — the little house was her birthday present. "We thought you'd like a place to get away from it all once in a while," her parents told her.

And it's been great. When we have our sleep-overs out there, we can play Video Trax as loud as we like, and talk and giggle all night long without bothering anybody. We also have a cordless phone if we get the urge to call anybody. There's even a refrigerator full of goodies like Dr Pepper and cheese dip.

The three of us were heading for the back door when Mrs. Green called from the house, "Who's that, Stephanie?"

"I'm surprised she even noticed," Stephanie muttered. "When she's with the twins, she's on another *planet*!" Then she called back, "It's Kate and Lauren, Mom."

"Would you girls like to see how much the babies have grown?" Mrs. Green said, poking her head out of the twins' bedroom. "You haven't gotten a peek at them since the day we brought them home from the hospital."

"Mom!" Stephanie groaned softly. Kate and I exchanged glances. For Stephanie's sake, we didn't want to seem too interested — we knew how *she* felt about the twins. On the other hand, it would be rude to say "No, thank you," to her mom.

"Sure, Mrs. Green," Kate said. "We'd love to."

"That'd be great," I added, even though babies all look pretty much alike to me.

"Terrific!" Stephanie grumbled. Her permanent frown deepened.

Kate and I tramped down the hall in our snow boots. Stephanie dragged along behind us.

The twins' bedroom looked just like a babies' department store. There were mobiles of stars, planets, fishes, and teddy bears dangling from the ceiling. Every inch of floor space was jammed with strollers, rocking horses, and giant stuffed animals.

Waving toward the two white cribs against the wall, Mrs. Green sang out, "Sweeties! You have company."

One of the cribs had a white cover with colored kites printed on it; the other had a yellow cover with boats. One twin had a little more hair, the other was larger. Both babies were round and chubby and barely had their eyes open.

"This is Jeremy." Mrs. Green pointed to the smaller twin with more hair, under the kite cover.

41

"And this is Emma." She turned to us. "Aren't they gorgeous?" she said proudly. She turned back and beamed at the babies.

Kate and I nodded. Stephanie sighed loudly and shuffled her feet. "Mom," she said in a sulky voice, "we're in kind of a hurry. . . ."

My mother would have gotten mad at me if I'd acted like that, but Mrs. Green didn't. "Go ahead, then," she said, giving Stephanie what I thought was kind of a concerned look.

"We've got stuff to do in the apartment," Stephanie said, softening a little.

"Have a good time," said Mrs. Green.

"See what I mean?" Stephanie muttered as she stalked down the hall. "On another planet!"

I didn't agree — I was sure Mrs. Green knew very well how Stephanie was feeling, and was worried about it. But I was also sure it wouldn't do any good to argue.

"Gorgeous?!" Stephanie went on. "Has Mom lost her eyesight? With that wrinkled red face, Jeremy looks like a monkey. And Emma looks like . . . like Todd Schwartz's bulldog!" Todd Schwartz is Stephanie's across-the-street neighbor.

42

Kate and I grinned at each other. It wasn't a very nice thing to say, but Emma *did* look a little like Bozo.

"Don't worry. She won't look that way forever," I told Stephanie. "Babies change a lot. Remember how hideous Lolly Norris was when she was little?" Lolly is a kid who lives at the end of the block. "She looked like something straight out of *Creature Features*. But she's okay-looking now."

Stephanie shrugged and frowned again.

Behind us, one of the twins started to howl.

"Let's get out of here before the other one tunes up!" Stephanie grabbed her jacket off a hook in the kitchen, and we scooted through the door. Then the three of us ran down the walk to Stephanie's apartment.

The apartment is basically one big room, with cabinets, a steel sink, and a little refrigerator against one wall. There's also a small bathroom in back. Naturally the apartment's decorated in shades of red, white, and black — Stephanie's favorite colors. There are two gray-and-white pull-out couches, a black metal table, a red-and-black tweed rug, and red curtains with tiny black-and-white squiggles.

As I pulled off my coat I said, "Looks like Ms. Gilberto's been here." Ms. Gilberto's the art teacher at Riverhurst Elementary.

There was a big pile of art supplies on the black metal table — Stephanie had thought of everything. There was a package of oversized gray construction paper, a bottle of rubber cement, three pairs of scissors, a ball of string, and a big handful of markers (mostly black and red ones, of course).

Kate pointed to a stack of white plastic dishes on the end of the couch. "For eating, or juggling?" she asked Stephanie.

"Trying to juggle," Stephanie sighed. "I'm afraid it's not going too well, though. Those plates spend a lot more time on the floor than they do in the air." She picked up a marker and started to doodle on a piece of gray paper. "I've been thinking," she continued gloomily. "As far as the party service goes, I'm not doing us any good at all. Lauren, you and Patti make excellent clowns. You can do all those flips and cartwheels and stuff. And Kate makes great videos." Stephanie put down the black marker and picked up a red one. "As far as I can tell, I don't add a single thing! I might as well give up. Then you can

44

split the profits among the three of you, instead of paying me for doing nothing."

Kate and I couldn't believe our ears.

"No way!" Kate argued. "You set up the scenes. You get all the kids together. You get them to relax in front of the camera and act natural. . . ."

"Big deal," Stephanie said. "So I'm good at pushing little kids around. You could manage without me. I'm just dead wood."

"Stephanie, why are you cutting yourself down like this?" I scolded.

"I'm not cutting myself down. I'm just being realistic," she replied in a low voice. "In the last couple of weeks, I've started facing facts. My parents always made me feel like a star. But now, with the twins around, I see that I'm really not that good at anything." Stephanie sighed again. "I'm just hopeless . . ."

Kate and I looked at each other. Stephanie sure was down! But neither of us knew what to do to cheer her up.

"Anyway, we'd better get moving on Kate's costume, or we'll never make the party at the Duvas' on time," Stephanie finished.

Kate took off her blue sweatpants. She had her gray tights on underneath. She pulled Stephanie's dad's gray sweater on over her sweatshirt. The sweater was huge. It covered her hands with at least eight inches of wool sleeve to spare.

"If you bunch up the extra sleeve, and squeeze it in your hands, it should look fat and flat, like elephants' feet," Stephanie said.

The bottom of the sweater hung well past Kate's knees. Stephanie suggested that we pad out the body by adding a few more sweatshirts, and maybe a pillow or two, underneath it.

It worked even better than we'd hoped. No one would ever guess that Kate Beekman was underneath that big gray ball of a body!

Even the elephant's head turned out to be easier to make than we expected. First we cut out a big circle for the face. Then we stapled to the bottom the grayish dryer hose I'd brought from home. It really looked like an elephant's trunk. After that we cut out two ears — each in the shape of half a big Valentine's heart — and taped them to opposite edges of the circle. We made holes for the elephant's eyes (and for Kate to see through). And as a finishing touch

Stephanie drew on eyelids and eyelashes with a black marker. Then we stapled strings on each side of the head so Kate could tie the mask around her head.

"I actually do look a little like an elephant," Kate said, peering at herself in the full-length mirror on the bathroom door. She sounded totally amazed.

"It's Lauren's dryer hose that really makes it," Stephanie said, even though *she* was the one who thought out the whole design.

We were adding more padding to the gray sweater, so that Kate's body would look absolutely round, when Patti finally showed up.

"I caught a ride from the library with Walter Williams and his mom," she said, huffing and puffing. "Then I ran up their back alley." The Williamses live on the other side of the Greens' back fence. Walter Williams is in the Quarks Club, too. He's another real brain.

"Did you find out anything about palm reading?" Kate asked her.

"I checked out a few books," Patti said, slapping her backpack. "I read about heart lines, head lines, fate lines, life lines . . . it gets pretty confusing, es-

47

pecially since they're different on every palm. And then all the little bumps on your hand are supposed to mean something, too," she added. She pulled off her mitten and studied her palm. "I can't keep it straight," she admitted. "I really think it might be too difficult for little kids to understand. Or care about. All Horace wants to know about the future is stuff like are we going to Burger Joint for dinner on Saturday, or is he going to get a snapping turtle for his next birthday."

"You may be right," Kate agreed.

"So palm reading is for grown-ups," I said. "And it's back to the old drawing board."

"No — out into the snow," Stephanie said. "It's already a quarter to two. We'd better get going."

We put the mask on Kate again. Then we added a gray wool hat to cover her blonde hair. Kate had worn her gray snow boots, and they made pretty good elephant hind feet. Her hands were hidden by eight inches of gray sweater sleeve and her body was more or less elephant-shaped. It really was a *terrific* costume!

"Kate, bend over a little, and walk so that your trunk sways from side to side . . . ," Patti advised. Kate did. Patti clapped. "Outstanding!"

"Just perfect!" Stephanie and I chimed in. We were all pleased with our work.

Stephanie wasn't even frowning anymore. In fact, the only person who wasn't happy was Kate. "I still can't believe I'm doing this!" She mumbled. "I don't know how you guys talked me into it!"

Chapter 5

The four of us left Stephanie's apartment and snuck around the Greens' back fence and into the Williamses' yard.

Patti started to giggle as we crept alongside their juniper hedge.

"What's so funny?" Stephanie whispered.

"It's not often that you see an elephant in the snow in Riverhurst!" Patti whispered back.

"Everybody take a good look," Kate muttered, "because it's the only time in this life you'll get to see *this* elephant!"

After the Williamses' comes the Murphys' house, then the Brunos', and finally the Duvas'. We crept from yard to yard. Finally we came to a halt behind the Duvas' garage. Their garage is to one side of their house, so by peering carefully around the corner of it, we could keep an eye on the front door *and* the back door.

There were already lots of cars pulling into the driveway, and lots of little kids getting out. They were all wearing costumes. There was a clown, a trapeze artist, an acrobat, and a magician. . . .

"A magician?!" I hissed, as someone in black disappeared into the house. "Do you think that was Mandrake, slipping through the back door? He was wearing a black cape, and he looked awfully tall for a second-grader to me!"

"Nuts! I missed him," Stephanie said. "I was too busy checking out the lion tamer."

She pointed to a little kid dressed in a bright red jumpsuit with a glittery gold mask and a matching belt. He was holding a whip in one hand, and he had a big toy lion draped across his shoulders. He looked very tough!

"I missed him, too," Patti said.

"And I didn't see anything!" Kate grumbled. "This mask keeps slipping!" She adjusted her elephant face and peered out of the eyeholes. "There's that twerp Freddie!" she growled.

51

Freddie Duva had marched out onto the front lawn to greet his guests. He was dressed as a circus ringmaster. He had on a white jacket, tight red pants stuffed into big (for Freddie) black boots, and a black top hat.

"I know who you are!" he bellowed at a little girl in a pink tutu and feathered mask. "You're Amy Munstead! Yuck! You look like a geek!"

"Maybe it's just as well we aren't doing this party," Patti murmured. "The birthday boy seems a wee bit critical."

"Charming!" Stephanie murmured.

"I'm freezing!" Kate complained. Her teeth were chattering. "You guys have no idea how drafty it is under this sweater."

"Why don't you go inside?" Patti suggested.

"Right — there are plenty of kids around now. Just mingle!" Stephanie directed.

"Mingle?" Kate said indignantly. Then she sighed. "Okay. Front door, or back?" she asked.

"Back. Mrs. Duva's bound to be easier to fool than old eagle-eye Freddie," I said. Stephanie and Patti nodded in agreement.

Kate waited until a big yellow station wagon pulled up in the driveway between us and the house.

Then she crept out from behind the garage and joined the crowd — she really didn't look out of place. She stooped so far over that her hands almost brushed against the sidewalk. Swaying her trunk from side to side, she started up the back steps.

Mrs. Duva walked out onto the back porch. "I just love your costume!" she said to Kate, holding the door open so Kate could lumber through it. "Who's under that mask? Is it Jimmy Metcalf? Or is it Brucie Rodwin?"

I half expected Kate to raise up and exclaim, "Brucie Rodwin?! Give me a break!" We've had plenty of problems with Brucie at other parties. In fact, Brucie Rodwin is probably just about Kate's least favorite kid of all time. But she managed to keep a grip on herself and wagged her big elephant head, slowly up and down.

"Home free," Patti whispered as Kate lurched into the house.

"Way to go!" Stephanie hissed excitedly.

"Now what?" I asked.

"We wait until Mandrake does his thing, and makes his exit," Stephanie explained. "Then we track him down!"

Crouching behind the Duvas' garage has to be

a lot more comfortable in the summer than it was in the middle of winter. The snow on the roof was melting a little, and every minute or so, a large drop of ice-water would land in our hair or on our noses. My fingers felt as though they were about to fall off.

Stephanie's lips were turning blue — not one of her favorite colors — and Patti's nose was bright red. To take our minds off the fact that we were all about to develop major cases of frostbite, we tried once again to figure out Magnificent Mandrake's real identity.

"What did the magician you saw look like?" Stephanie asked me.

I shrugged. "I only got a two-second look before he went inside," I said. "He was kind of skinny, with a long head."

"Charlie Garner?" Patti asked. Charlie's in the Video Club with Kate and Stephanie.

"Charlie's built like a fire hydrant," Stephanie said, shaking her head.

We came up with about eight more names after that, but none of them seemed right. Mandrake's identity was as much of a mystery as ever. Then we heard the kids in the Duvas' house singing: "Happy birthday, dear Freddie. . . ."

"If they're singing now, there's the cake and presents to get through before they even start with Mandrake!" Stephanie said, with a shiver. "We'll be frozen solid by then! I vote we wait inside the garage — we'll still have a good view."

"What if somebody catches us in there?" Patti asked.

"Who's going to catch us? They're all at the party," Stephanie said. "And if they do, we'll just tell them we're . . . looking for Cinders! Come on!"

The garage door was slightly open. The three of us slipped through it and stamped our feet to knock some of the snow off our boots.

"This is definitely an improvement," Patti said, clapping her hands together.

I rubbed my tingling ears with my mittens. "It feels about fifty degrees warmer," I agreed.

"Wow!" Stephanie said. "Look at all that stuff!" She pointed at a long wooden shelf running across the back wall.

"Old magazines!" Patti cried. She squeezed between the Duvas' two cars to get to the shelf. "This is great!" She picked up a copy of *Natural Science Monthly*.

"And there are comics, too!" I said, grabbing

three or four issues of *Creature Features*. "Freddie can't be all bad."

"Pull up a chair," Stephanie said, motioning to an overturned wheelbarrow and a big bag of peat moss.

"Shouldn't we be looking out the window for Mandrake?" Patti asked.

"Don't worry about it," Stephanie said. "It'll be thirty minutes, at least, before anything happens."

She settled down on the wheelbarrow with an old issue of *Style* magazine — her favorite. Patti and I shared the bag of peat moss.

The three of us had been reading for a while when Patti whispered, "Hey, you guys, we're not alone!"

"Is somebody coming?" Stephanie hissed.

Patti shook her head and pointed. A scraggly, brown dog lay stretched out in the far corner. He was fast asleep. He was the kind of big, shabby-looking dog you see all over the place and never look at twice.

"Not very pretty, is he?" Patti said as the dog raised his long, narrow head and yawned in our direction.

"I didn't even know the Duvas had a dog,"

Stephanie mumbled. She looked back down at her magazine. "He's not much of a guard dog, is he? He looks too lazy to bite!"

That's when the big dog sat bolt upright. In a flash he scrambled to his feet, dashed between the two cars, and burst through the garage door like a rocket.

"Whoa!" Stephanie cried. She dropped her *Style* magazine and rushed to the window.

"What's going on?" I asked, jumping up from my comfortable peat-moss cushion.

"That's Mandrake's dog!" Stephanie shrieked. "Hurry, or we'll lose them!"

Chapter
6

I don't think I've ever run so hard in my life! Patti and I have much longer legs than Stephanie, so we soon left her far behind.

We chased Mandrake and the brown dog down the Duvas' driveway, across Clearview Crescent, and back. Then we chased them around the Murphys' yard and up the Williamses' alley. That's when he managed to give us the slip. Mandrake had left his bicycle propped up against the Williamses' side fence. Just as we were about to catch up with him, he jumped on his bike, pedaled madly down the alley, and disappeared up the street. The big brown dog was right at his heels.

"Whew!" I collapsed onto the Willises' trash

cans, gasping for breath. "Were you close enough to get a good look at him?" I asked Patti. She'd been a little ahead of me at one point.

Patti shook her head. "The hat and the black cape covered everything the mask didn't," she panted. "Still, I can't help feeling there was something kind of familiar about him. . . ."

Stephanie finally caught up with us, and Kate arrived about thirty seconds later. She'd lost her trunk in the Williamses' hedge, and she was carrying her elephant mask under her arm. She was also carrying a wooden giraffe party-favor, and a small silver trophy.

"What's that for?" Stephanie wheezed, pointing at the trophy.

"For best costume, thank you very much," Kate puffed. "I beat out the lion tamer, who threw a temper tantrum. Talk about feeling ridiculous. It's a good thing I left when I did, too. It was almost time for us to take off our masks to play pin the tail on the donkey!"

The four of us started to giggle. "Mrs. Duva would have been very surprised to discover you weren't Jimmy Metcalf after all," Patti said.

"Not to mention Brucie Rodwin!" I added.

"Let's go back to the apartment," Stephanie said, still puffing. "I want to get something to drink."

"And I want to get something to eat," I chimed in.

"Yeah, I'm starving!" Kate said. "I only had a couple of bites of cake. Chocolate, with white icing — in the shape of a circus tent."

"Well, how was Mandrake?" Stephanie asked Kate when we got inside. She handed Kate and me an extra-large bag of cheese curls. "Was he any good?"

Kate threw her mask on the table and pulled off the big, gray sweater. "Unfortunately, he was excellent. He did all the tricks Freddie had told his mother about, plus card tricks. He also made a gerbil appear out of a ball of wadded-up newspaper and gave the gerbil to Freddie. It was a nice touch. The kids thought Mandrake was the greatest," Kate added gloomily.

"Do you have any idea who he is?" I asked.

Kate shook her head. "He had on his hat and his mask, of course. He also hardly ever faced the audience. He used that phony, deep voice of his, too, with a really hokey Dracula-type accent."

"So how are we going to find out who he is?"

Stephanie asked, glancing around at Kate, Patti, and me. "Search for that brown dog of his?"

"There must be brown dogs just like that on practically every block in Riverhurst," Kate said. We looked at each other glumly.

Patti was sitting at the table. She picked up what was left of the elephant mask and held it up to her face. All of a sudden, she exclaimed, "Who did these?"

"Who did what?" Kate, Stephanie, and I asked.

"These drawings! They're wonderful!" Patti replied, pointing to the underside of one of the elephant ears.

Stephanie took a look. "Oh, I was just doodling on the construction paper," she said. Then she actually *blushed*. "Tear them up."

Stephanie made a grab for the ear, but Patti pulled the mask out of her reach.

"Let's see!" Kate and I said, crowding closer. Then we both cracked up.

"They're hysterical!" Kate said.

Using black and red markers, Stephanie had drawn pictures of both of the twins. "It looks just like them!" I cried. And it did, only funnier. Jeremy looked like Jeremy, but he also looked like a little monkey with a wrinkled, red face. You could recognize Emma, too, with her thin hair and big eyes. But she also looked a lot like Todd Schwartz's bulldog, Bozo.

"I didn't know you could draw, Stephanie," I said. I was really surprised. She's never been especially good in art class, but then she usually just makes collages because Ms. Gilberto once yelled at her for spilling poster paint all over the place.

"I can't," Stephanie insisted. "These are just doodles, turning people into animals."

"Do us!" I begged.

Stephanie shook her head and blushed again. "I really can't," she said.

"Come on! Try it!" Kate directed.

We sat Stephanie down at the table with her markers, while Patti, Kate, and I faced her on the couch. Stephanie stared at each of us hard. First she frowned. Then she started to grin. She picked up a black marker and began drawing furiously on a piece of gray construction paper.

When Stephanie was done, she didn't want to show us the results, but Kate snatched the paper away from her. Kate took a quick look at it and burst out laughing. She held up the paper for Patti and me to see, too.

Stephanie had drawn Kate as a combination of her real self and a fox. Kate's blonde hair was brushed back into two little fox ears; her face was a fox's face, with a pointy nose and a neat, narrow little head. It looked just right.

Patti was a squirrel, with bright eyes that were intelligent and watchful. And I was a cocker spaniel, with long, furry ears and a kind of dreamy expression.

"That's me, all right," I said.

Kate giggled. "Yeah, just before you decide you've spotted a UFO in the backyard!" She loves to tease me about my runaway imagination.

"These are really outstanding, Stephanie," Patti said.

Kate nodded. "I think we've just added a new feature to the Sleepover Friends Party Service — Caricatures by Stephanie Green, Artist."

"Oh, no!" Stephanie shook her head. "These are just doodles. I'm not an artist!" She looked at us suspiciously. "You guys are just saying that to cheer me up, right?"

Kate, Patti, and I shook our heads. But I could

tell Stephanie didn't believe us — she had on that "I'm no good at anything" expression again.

"Let me see your hands," Patti ordered.

"My hands?" Stephanie repeated, puzzled.

Patti reached for Stephanie's hands and turned them over. She studied the palms for a minute. "Hmmm . . ." she said. Then she traced some of the lines on Stephanie's palm with her fingers. "You're daring and ambitious," she began in a serious voice. "And this" — Patti tapped the bump just under Stephanie's little finger — "is the Mount of Mercury. Yours is large, which means you're *very* creative and artistic. All the great artists in history had large Mounts of Mercury — Picasso, Van Gogh. . . ."

Stephanie's mouth dropped open. "Really?" She studied her hand thoughtfully. "I'm sure it doesn't mean a thing. . . ." But she sounded kind of impressed.

Kate glanced at the clock above the sink. "Four-thirty!"

"My mom will be here any minute!" Patti said. "We're all going to the mall for an early dinner at Burger Joint." She looked over at Kate and me. "Do you guys want a ride?"

Kate nodded. "Sure. I was going to call my dad, but this'll save him a trip."

"Yeah — thanks," I agreed.

We pulled on our coats. Kate turned to Stephanie. "Practice your drawings," she said with a grin. "We have to get an ad together to put in the *Clarion* by Wednesday. I can just see it: 'Dazzling Caricatures, by Stephanie!' "

"Get serious!" Stephanie said, making a face. But she was still studying her palm when we left, and I thought she looked a lot happier than she had since the twins came home from the hospital.

After Kate, Patti, and I had piled into the back of Mrs. Jenkins' station wagon, I said, "Patti, would you mind checking out my palm, like you did for Stephanie?"

Patti coughed and looked sort of embarrassed. "Remember what Kate said about one of us being an undercover Pinocchio? Well, I feel like I have."

"What's that supposed to mean?" Kate asked her.

"Well . . . I was afraid my nose would start to grow back there," Patti whispered because she didn't want her mom to hear. "The truth is, I don't really know anything about palmistry yet. I made it all up."

"About the Mount of Mercury and artists and everything?" I said. "You *didn't*, Patti?!" I was flabbergasted. Patti Jenkins does not usually run around telling fibs!

Patti nodded and sighed.

"That's okay. It was for a good cause," Kate said approvingly. Mrs. Jenkins had stopped the car in front of my house, and Kate opened the door.

"Stephanie's drawings *were* great," Patti said. "All she needed was some confidence, and she seems to have lost hers since the twins came." She smiled sheepishly. "I figured a little bit of pretend palm reading wouldn't hurt." She waved at us as the car pulled away. "See you on Monday!"

Chapter
7

Patti's palm reading must have done Stephanie's confidence some good. When the four of us met before school on Monday at the corner of Pine and Hillcrest, Stephanie seemed more like her old self. Her frown was gone, and she had a little red sketchbook full of drawings to show us.

"Leather?" I asked about the sketchbook.

Stephanie nodded, handing it over. "My dad noticed me sketching on Saturday, so he bought it for me on his trip to Romanos yesterday."

I opened the book to the first page, and burst into giggles. "Jenny Carlin, as a Siamese cat!" I announced, holding up the picture. It was perfect. Jenny was wearing her famous pink jumpsuit. With her button nose and big round eyes, and arched eyebrows she looked exactly like a snooty Siamese.

Kate took the notebook from me. "This is great!" she said. "Angela Kemp as a lumpy old dog . . . and Mrs. Wainwright as a penguin!" Kate cracked up as she turned the pages.

"Speaking of dogs, isn't this the dog we saw in the Duvas' garage?" Patti said, pointing to a drawing of a sleepy-looking mutt with a long, narrow head and pointy ears.

Stephanie nodded. "Mandrake's dog. You know how people say dogs often look a lot like their owners? Well, that dog reminds me of *somebody*. I just haven't figured out who yet."

"These are terrific, Stephanie," I said, flipping through the sketchbook again. "Hey — isn't this Jeremy?"

On the next-to-last page of the book, Stephanie had drawn the smaller twin. He didn't look nearly as much like a wrinkled-up little monkey as he had in the Saturday sketch. Jeremy's hair was combed down, his eyes were wide open, and his mouth was turned up at the corners.

"Yeah." Stephanie glanced at the drawing. "He

actually smiled at me while I was doing it, can you believe it?'' And she definitely sounded pleased.

Stephanie turned the page over. ''Here's Emma.''

Emma was lying on her back in her crib, waving her chubby arms and legs in the air. ''From this angle, she looks a lot less like Bozo Schwartz,'' Stephanie murmured, tracing the sketch with her finger. ''Mom wants me to make larger drawings from these. She's going to have them framed at Art-a-rama, and hang them in the living room.''

Kate and Patti and I grinned at each other.

''Way to go, Stephanie!'' I said. And way to go, Mr. and Mrs. Green, I added to myself.

''It's eight-thirty already,'' Kate said, glancing at her watch. ''We'd better step on it, or we'll be having lunch with a penguin.'' At Riverhurst Elementary, if you're late more than once a semester, you have to spend your lunch hour in the principal's office. And believe me, it isn't a treat.

We got on our bikes and started pedaling.

''I guess it doesn't really matter anymore who Mandrake is,'' Patti said as we coasted downhill toward school. ''Who cares about his magic tricks? The

Sleepover Friends have an artist on their team!"

"*I* care!" Kate exclaimed. "Mandrake is taking away our business!"

Stephanie agreed. "Besides, anybody who is so sneaky deserves to be found out," she said. "Why did he run away from us like that, anyway?" She added sternly. "A guilty conscience!"

We locked our bikes up in the racks in front of the school building and hurried up the walk. Just as we got to the front steps, Jenny Carlin and Robert Ellwanger came face-to-face for the first time since our Friday-night phone call.

"Hi, Jenny," Robert squeaked, pulling nervously at the neck of his saggy brown sweater. "I'm sorry I couldn't make it on Saturday. . . ."

Unluckily for Robert, Henry Larkin and Larry Jackson and some of the other guys were hanging around the steps, too. "Yo, Jenny!" Henry said with a big grin. "I didn't know you and *Bob* Ellwanger here were — "

"What are you talking about?!" Jenny screeched at Robert in a voice practically hard enough to cut glass. She was wearing the turquoise jacket with the fake-fur hood she thinks is so glamorous, and boy was she *mad*.

70

"Going over to your house last Saturday after-noon . . . ," Robert said. He should have known enough to just let it drop.

"Have you lost your mind?!" Jenny screeched even louder. "*Me* ask *you* over? Get real, Robert Ellwanger!" Then she swept through the doors, with Angela tagging along behind her just like the big, lumpy dog Stephanie had drawn.

Robert stood there for a second, with a stunned look on his face. Then he saw Kate, Patti, Stephanie, and me watching him. He turned and ran around to the side door.

"Robert Ellwanger never knows when to quit," Kate said as we headed up the hall toward 5B. "I'm almost sorry we set him up," she added, which is as close as Kate ever gets to sounding regretful.

"Uh-hmmm," Patti said, her mind somewhere else. Then we walked into our classroom.

As soon as we sat down, Stephanie sketched something in her little red book. And she kept on sketching in it, right under Mrs. Mead's nose, all the way through math and on into social studies. It made me nervous. I was sure she'd get caught. After all, Stephanie sits in the front row. (Kate and I sit in the second, right behind her.)

Finally, just after Mrs. Mead told us to take out our science notebooks and turn to Chapter Ten: Stars and Planets, I heard Stephanie exclaim under her breath, "That's it!"

"Do you have something you'd like to share with the rest of the class, Stephanie?" Mrs. Mead asked. She frowned at Stephanie from behind her desk.

"No, Mrs. Mead," Stephanie said quickly. "Sorry."

But as soon as Mrs. Mead went up to the board, Stephanie quietly tore a page out of her sketchbook. While Mrs. Mead was busy writing facts about red giants, white dwarves, and other kinds of stars on the blackboard, Stephanie folded the paper into a tiny square. Then she stuck her left hand behind her, as though she were scratching her back, and dropped the square of paper on the floor in front of me. I dropped my pencil, on purpose. When I leaned down to pick it up, I scooped up Stephanie's square of paper, too.

I unfolded it in my lap, a little at a time, so that Mrs. Mead wouldn't notice. But when I'd finally gotten it completely unfolded and smoothed out so I could actually see what was on it, I gasped out loud — I couldn't help myself!

I tried to cover the gasp with a cough. Then I stared down at the paper again. First there was a picture of Mandrake's big brown dog, looking just like he had in the Duvas' garage. Next to it, Stephanie had sketched Robert Ellwanger. Robert and the dog were both skinny, with these long heads, pointy ears, and big feet.

In the third drawing Robert's face and the dog's face were kind of blended into each other — it was fantastic — and the fourth drawing was of Mandrake. He was all in black, with a hat and cape on, but no mask. And Mandrake was Robert Ellwanger! Robert Ellwanger?!

Why not? He was tall enough. He was definitely skinny enough. Robert's an only child, so he wouldn't have to worry about a little brother or sister giving him away. He wouldn't have to worry about friends giving him away either — the poor guy doesn't really have any friends. And having no friends means he'd have lots of free time to learn magic tricks. If Robert Ellwanger were Mandrake that would also explain why he'd turned Jenny Carlin down last Saturday! It *had* to be him!

Kate nudged me, so I passed the paper to her under our desks. I pretended to gaze up at Mrs.

Mead, who was still at the blackboard talking about the birth and death of stars. But I was really watching Kate out of the corner of my eye. First she raised an eyebrow as high as it could go. Then she stared at the drawing so hard her eyes looked like they were going to pop out of her head. Finally she poked Stephanie with her big toe and nodded, just once. Obviously, Kate was pretty sure Stephanie was right, too!

I could hardly wait until lunch so we could show Patti the drawings. Patti sits at the back of the room, in the very last row, so there wasn't a *hope* of passing the drawings to her during class.

As soon as the lunch bell rang, though, and we filed out into the hall, Stephanie, Kate, and I grabbed Patti. We pulled her over to the wall near the water fountain.

"We think we know who Mandrake is!" I whispered excitedly. The other kids in 5B were whizzing past us, trying to be first in line in the cafeteria.

"Right, we're pretty sure Mandrake is — " Stephanie began.

But Patti interrupted her, "Remember how I said there was something kind of familiar about Mandrake, after we'd chased him?'' she asked. Without giving any of us a chance to answer, she went on, ''I figured out what it was! The way he ran reminded me of Kate's puppets, throwing their arms and legs around, and Kate's puppets reminded us of . . .''

''Robert Ellwanger!'' all four of us hissed at once. Kate pulled out Stephanie's drawings and held them in front of Patti's face.

''Move along, girls,'' Mrs. Mead called from the door of 5B, waving her hand at us. We started up the hall again.

''Wow,'' Patti said, shaking her head sort of disbelievingly. ''So you guys think so, too.''

''And to imagine I was actually feeling sorry for that creep, not three hours ago!'' Kate growled. ''Robert Ellwanger is the reason I had to dress up like an elephant and make a total fool of myself, crashing a second-grader's party!''

''Well, you *did* win a trophy,'' Stephanie pointed out with a giggle.

''What are we going to do about him?'' I asked as we stepped through the cafeteria doors.

''I'll tell you what I'd like to do,'' Kate said. ''I'd

75

like to find him right now and . . . and. . . .''

"Calm down, Kate." Patti cut in. "We have to be cool about this. We *could* be wrong, you know. If we act too fast we could really end up looking like jerks."

We all quieted down. Patti had a point. We pushed our trays through the cafeteria line, and loaded up our plates with the special of the day — franks and beans, and raspberry-lime Jell-O — a dessert that doesn't even thrill *me* much. Then we headed for our regular table.

"Where does Robert Ellwanger live?" Stephanie asked when we'd sat down.

"On McIlhenny, I think," Patti said. "I went there with my dad once, to visit Mr. Gibbs" — Mr. Gibbs is head of the history department at the university, where both of Patti's parents are professors — "and I saw Robert hanging out in the yard across the street."

"So we'll ride our bikes over there after school," I said. "And if we find the brown dog, then we'll definitely know if Robert Ellwanger *is* Mandrake!"

Kate shook her head. "It won't prove anything. Robert Ellwanger could always say his *dog* might have been at the Duvas' on Saturday, but he wasn't

76

anywhere near there. We have to catch him in the act.''

"That's easy!" I said. "We'll keep his house under surveillance until he leaves for a party wearing the Mandrake outfit. Then we'll jump out and nab him!"

"Lau-ren!" Kate said with a sigh. "You've been watching too many cop shows on TV! That could take forever!"

"Besides, we'd freeze to death!" Stephanie said, with a shiver. "Why don't we just call the number in the *Clarion*, and leave a message asking him to entertain at a party at my house! Then when he gets there, we. . . ."

"That wouldn't work, either," Patti broke in. "Once Robert found out where he was going, he wouldn't show up. If he *is* Mandrake, he knows we're after him. We chased him all over Riverhurst — remember?"

"She's right," Kate said. "We'll just have to waylay him on his way to his next party."

"But how will we find out where and when it is?" Stephanie asked. "I'm not exactly up on the first- and second-grade social calendar."

Kate giggled. "You'll just have to ask every little

kid you see," she said. "Sshhh — *here comes our main Mandrake suspect now. . . ."*

The four of us stared daggers at Robert Ellwanger as he strolled as casually as he could across the cafeteria, and sat by himself near the window.

Chapter
8

As it turned out, the *first* little kid we asked knew about Mandrake's next party. It was Horace, Patti's little brother, and he told us everything we wanted to know that very afternoon.

Kate, Stephanie, and I rode our bikes over to Patti's house after school that day. Patti and her mom were repainting Patti's bedroom in a really pretty peach color. The three of us were going to help.

We'd brought our oldest jeans and buttoned some old shirts of Mr. Jenkins's over our regular tops. We were busy pushing all of Patti's furniture into the middle of the room when Horace came clattering up the stairs. Horace is an okay kid — okay, that is, for a pint-sized six-year-old with a giant-sized IQ.

"Hey!" Horace said, peeking through the door at us.

"Hey, Horace," Stephanie, Kate, and I replied.

"Let's ask him about Mandrake!" Stephanie suggested.

"You mean, Magnificent Mandrake, the magician?" Horace volunteered. "He's supposed to be great. I'm seeing him tomorrow!"

"Tomorrow?!" Stephanie repeated excitedly. "Where?"

"And when?" Patti put in quickly.

"He's going to be at Bonnie Fizer's birthday," Horace said. "After school at her house. Bonnie doesn't know. It's a surprise party!"

Kate let out a low whistle. "Bonnie's not the only one who's going to be surprised," she said grimly.

Elementary school gets out at three o'clock. According to Horace, Bonnie's party was officially supposed to start at four. But Bonnie's mother had asked the other little kids to get there fifteen minutes earlier, to give them time to hide in the house. Then Mrs. Fizer would bring Bonnie home from a fast visit to the mall. When they came through the door, everybody would jump out and scream "Surprise!" as loud as they could. That was the part Horace was really looking forward to.

They'd all sing "Happy Birthday," and Mandrake would do his magic tricks *before* the cake. Mrs. Fizer's mother had explained to Mrs. Jenkins that if Mandrake went on *after* the cake, the kids might get so excited they'd all get sick. Kate scowled when she heard that. It didn't make me feel so great either. Sparkly and Barkly certainly didn't have that strong an effect.

The four of us decided we'd better get to the Fizers' house by three-thirty, and get ourselves settled before anybody else — especially Mandrake — showed up.

"No way will that sneak escape us this time," Kate said, with a determined look. "This time we've got him!"

The Fizers live at the very end of Lindenwood Circle in an old house surrounded by evergreen bushes and tall trees. We dragged our bikes behind two huge pines, and made our plans.

"Lauren, you and I will check out the back," Kate said in a low voice.

"Meanwhile Patti and I will crawl into those azalea bushes, and keep an eye on the front," Stephanie said.

Kate and I crept through the trees and into the backyard. The Fizers's house had a big front door, a side door that opened onto the kitchen, and a back door that led to the basement. There was also a small gardening shed and a locked garage off to the side.

"The shed is the best place to hide," Kate murmured. "That way we can keep watch on the back of the house, and on the driveway, too."

"Sounds okay to me," I said.

We tried the shed door to make sure we could open it — we could. Then we snuck around the house to report back to Stephanie and Patti.

"We'll be in the shed in the backyard," Kate told them. "Now, take a whistle," she said, handing Stephanie one — she'd borrowed two plastic whistles from Melissa's room that morning. "If Mandrake shows up in front, whistle! If he shows up in back, we'll do the same."

"Here comes a car . . . ," I warned, pointing down the street at a slow-moving, gray van.

"Let's go . . . ," Kate said.

We scrambled out of the azaleas, crouched down, and dashed for the backyard. Then we flung ourselves into the shed.

We were just in time, because the van turned into the Fizers's driveway and stopped. The door opened and out came the Reese twins with their mother. They disappeared into the side door of the house.

We left the shed door open a crack, and peered out at the traffic in the driveway. We saw Larry Jackson's little brother, Jud; Henry Larkin's cousin, Susan; Horace and Mrs. Jenkins; and a whole bunch of other little kids come driving up.

"It looks like they've invited every five- and six-year-old in town," I murmured to Kate. "What time is it?"

Kate pushed back her jacket sleeve to look at her watch. She started to answer, but I clapped my mitten over her mouth. Then I put my finger to my lips and pointed. The shed door was slowly swinging open!

The two of us backed noiselessly away from the door, farther into the shed, and waited. . . . Soon a thin brown snout appeared in the crack, then two beady eyes, joined by a pair of pointed, German-shepherd-type ears — it was the brown dog!

The dog gave Kate and me a totally disinterested glance, walked to the back of the shed, and flopped down on the floor. He was ready for his birthday-party nap!

"If he's here, Mandrake can't be very far away!" Kate barely breathed in my ear.

We scooted forward, toward the shed door, and cautiously peeked out. Sure enough, there was Mandrake, dressed all in black, with a tall black hat and a big black cape! He had his back to us, and he was strolling toward the side door of the Fizers's house. He looked as if he didn't have a worry in the world. Little did he know what was coming!

Kate exploded out of the shed. "Where do you think you're going, Mandrake?!" she said in a loud voice.

Mandrake jumped about two feet in the air, and swung around. Naturally, he was wearing his black mask, too. He took one look at Kate and me, and sprinted toward the front yard, his cape flapping behind him.

"Wwwhhheeeett!" Kate blew Melissa's whistle, as hard as she could.

Three seconds later, Mandrake came racing back with Stephanie and Patti hot on his heels. Mandrake swerved toward the bushes at the last minute. I guess he planned to crash through them into the yard next door.

That's when Kate yelled, "Hold it right there, *Robert Ellwanger!*"

When he heard that, he stopped running and slumped down against a tree stump. He looked around at all of us. "Please don't tell anybody, okay?" he pleaded.

"Why shouldn't we?" Stephanie asked.

"Not even five-year-olds want a known geek for a magician," Robert mumbled.

"Get down!" Patti said. "Here come the Fizers. We don't want to ruin Bonnie's surprise!"

Bonnie's surprise party went off without a hitch. We dived into the evergreens before the Fizers drove up the driveway. And we insisted that Robert do his magic show as planned. It wouldn't be fair to disappoint Bonnie Fizer or Horace or any of the other little kids.

While we sat in the azalea bushes, waiting for

Robert to finish, the four of us talked over the whole situation.

"I really feel sorry for him." Patti said. "I mean, did you listen to what he said?"

"He actually called himself a geek!" Stephanie exclaimed. "Isn't that the worst?!" She looked sad.

"It's terrible when people are hard on themselves," Kate said pointedly, glancing at Stephanie. "But let's get back to the real question. What do we want from Robert Ellwanger in exchange for keeping quiet?"

"I guess we can't ask him to go out of the party business," I said. "It just wouldn't be fair. Besides, he needs the money to pay for his magic supplies, just like we need the money to pay for our video camera."

"Remember what you said about Henry Larkin, Lauren — that if he were Mandrake, he'd go into business *with* us?" Patti said. "What about giving that a try?"

"Ick!" Stephanie said. "Going into business with Robert Ellwanger? Gross me out!"

"Hold on . . . ," Kate said thoughfully. "If we keep on this way, we'll be competing with him, and we'll definitely lose customers." Kate's voice trailed off. We knew she was right. With Magnificent Mandrake still in business, we'd be lucky to keep half our customers. "But," Kate went on, "if Robert Ellwanger joins us, we'll get even more jobs, because the older kids like Mandrake, too."

"Then we'd have Sparkly and Barkly, an artist, *and* a magician," I said.

"Right," Kate said. "We could even charge more money."

"More money. . . ," Stephanie murmured. "You know what?" she added enthusiastically. "It really isn't a bad idea!"

Kate looked at her curiously. "You seem awfully cheerful, Stephanie," she said. "Aren't the terrible twosome driving you crazy anymore?"

Stephanie pulled a leaf off the azalea bush. "Actually," she mumbled, "I'm sort of changing my mind about the twins. . . ."

"What's that supposed to mean?" Kate asked.

"I think Stephanie means that she's gotten to like the twins after all," Patti said softly.

"Jeremy and Emma are really kind of cute," Stephanie admitted. "Especially when they smile. And they seem very smart for their age," she added defensively, with a glance at Kate's "just wait until they're older" expression. "And, after all, they *are* my sister and brother."

Patti and I grinned at each other. I had a feeling it wouldn't be too long before Stephanie was as proud of the twins as Mr. and Mrs. Green were.

"So how would our ad in the *Clarion* go?" I asked, changing the subject before we started getting too soppy. " 'Sleepover Friends Party Services: Sparkly and Barkly, World-famous Clowns. . . .' "

" 'Dazzling Caricatures by Stephanie . . . ,' " Patti added.

" 'Amazing Feats by Magnificent Mandrake the Magician,' " Kate went on.

" 'Expertly videotaped by K. Beekman!' " Stephanie ended. "It's perfect! Let's do it!"

Chapter 9

Stephanie turned out to be a lot easier to convince than Robert Ellwanger. I think Robert was hoping we'd get tired of waiting for him in the Fizers's azalea bushes, and forget the whole thing. After he'd finished his act, he slipped out the back door of the house and softly called for his dog: "Brownie! Brownie?!" When the four of us popped up as well, Robert got pretty grumpy.

"You're still here?!" He lifted his mask a little to scowl at us, then snapped it back into place.

"We're still here," Kate said. "And we've been thinking things over. . . ."

"You know how there are basically only two party businesses in Riverhurst for little kids?" Stephanie broke in. "Yours . . . and ours . . ."

". . . and how we take business away from you?" Patti went on — she didn't sound entirely certain about that part. "And the other way around?"

"So what do you want to do?" Robert interrupted. "Divide the town up? It would be fine with me." He shifted uneasily from foot to foot and looked down at his watch. "No," Kate said firmly. "We've decided that the only smart thing to do is join forces!" That got Robert's attention, all right.

"Wha-at?!" he exclaimed. He was actually offended. "Listen! I've worked hard to put together a really classy magic act." I noticed Robert didn't sound nearly as pitiful now as he had earlier that afternoon. "You don't seriously think I'm going to hook up with a couple of clowns, do you? No way!"

"*And* an artist!" I pointed out huffily. Why did everybody have to dump on Sparkly and Barkly all the time?

"Forget it! It's out of the question!" Robert Ellwanger said angrily. "You want money to keep quiet? I'll give you what I made this afternoon."

He threw back his big black cape and started to reach into his pocket, but Stephanie stopped him. "We don't want your money," she said firmly. "The question is, do you want everybody at Riverhurst Elementary to know who Mandrake the Magician is, or not?'' She squared her shoulders and stared him right in the eye. "Don't forget, I'm the reporter for 'Social Notes' on the school newspaper.''

It took just a second for Robert to think about it. He raised his hands in the air and mumbled, "It's a hold-up.'' Then he lowered them. "I guess you girls got me,'' he said in his phony Mandrake voice. Then he clutched at his heart and pretended to fall to the ground, dead.

"I'm glad you see it our way,'' Kate said briskly as Robert picked himself up and dusted off his cape. "We'll be putting an ad in the *Clarion* tomorrow. But first we have to decide whose telephone number to give.''

Stephanie nodded. "Is that your own private number, Robert? The one listed in the paper?'' she asked.

"Yeah,'' Robert nodded glumly. "Unlisted. I got it for my birthday.''

"Why don't we use that one, then?'' Stephanie said to Patti, Kate, and me. "That way we'll never miss a call, because Robert has an answering machine.''

"Of course, you'll have to redo the message," Kate told Robert. "It should say something like, 'This is the Sleepover Friends Party Service, the home of . . .' "

"*The Sleepover Friends Party Service!*" Robert exploded. "I won't do it!"

"Yes, you will," Stephanie said.

"Okay, okay," Robert growled. "I'll do it. But I have to get home now — all right?"

"So do we," Patti said.

"We'll try your number later to check," Kate called out as Robert disappeared into the trees behind us.

I did phone Mandrake after dinner that evening. The spooky music was gone, and Mandrake's deep, hollow voice sounded a little rusty. "Hello," he said, "this is Magnificent Mandrake the Magician . . ." Well he did put himself first! ". . . speaking for the Sleepover Friends Party Service. . . ." It sounded as though he could hardly force the words out. ". . . the home of Magnificent Mandrake the Magician, dazzling caricatures by Stephanie, those clever cut-ups, Sparkly and Barkly. . . ." Clever cut-ups? Kate must have given Robert further instructions.

92

Robert started to mumble toward the end, but he managed to get the whole message out, even about Kate's videotaping. The new, improved Sleepover Friends Party Service was in business!

Stephanie, Patti, Kate, and I put an ad in the *Clarion* the next afternoon. But before the paper had even come out, we got our first job. Robert told us about it at school first thing Thursday morning.

"Angela Kemp's mother called the number last night," he said in a low voice as we locked our bikes up in the rack.

"Angela Kemp!" I made a face, but Kate said, "Never mind, Lauren. It's a job, isn't it?"

"The ventriloquist they'd hired from Dannerville for Angela's little sister's party has a sore throat, and they need a quick replacement," Robert went on.

"Who did they want?" Patti asked him.

"Everybody," Robert answered gloomily.

"When?" Kate said.

"Tomorrow at four," Robert replied.

"Well, well!" a voice screeched practically at our elbows. "If it isn't a meeting of the Sleepover Friends Party Service." Jenny Carlin was standing there with Angela Kemp. "I guess that means you four know who the mysterious Mandrake is!" Jenny went on, ignoring Robert completely.

"What if we do?" Stephanie asked.

"I saw him leaving the Waxmans' party last week," Jenny said. "He looked totally cool. I'm dying to find out who he *really* is. I fully intend to check him out at Angela's tomorrow, along with the rest of you clowns." She smirked at us unpleasantly. Angela nodded her head up and down like a wind-up toy.

Robert had disappeared into the crowd of kids heading into the school building, safely out of range of Jenny Carlin's sharp eyes. But he wouldn't find it so easy to escape at Wanda Kemp's birthday party.

When we got to the Kemps' the next after-noon — their house is on Tuckahoe Road, not far from Patti's — our old friend the brown dog was al-ready there, taking his birthday-party nap on their driveway.

"That means Robert's somewhere close," Steph-anie said.

"I hope he's being careful," Patti added in a worried voice. "Jenny's definitely on his trail."

We leaned our bikes against the front porch and walked up to the house. We looked around when

94

we got inside, but we didn't see Jenny or Angela anywhere.

"Maybe they've gone shopping," Stephanie murmured hopefully. Jenny is about the only person in the world who's as nuts about shopping as Stephanie is.

Mrs. Kemp showed Patti and me where the bathroom was, so we could put on our clown makeup while Kate set up the video camera in the kitchen, and Stephanie organized her sketchpad and markers.

We'd already decided that Mandrake would go on first, with his magic tricks. Then he would sneak away, while Patti and I did our act and Mrs. Kemp carried out the cake. Stephanie would sketch the kids as Wanda, the birthday girl, opened her presents. And, naturally, Kate would videotape the whole thing.

By the time Patti and I had finished with our costumes, and gone into the kitchen, most of the guests had arrived. The kids were sitting around the big round table in the dining room. Kate took her place in a far corner with the video camera. At one minute to four, Mandrake crept through the Kemps' back door.

He shrugged his shoulders questioningly at Patti

and me. We shook our heads, meaning we hadn't seen Jenny or Angela anywhere. So Robert/Mandrake stepped bravely through the kitchen door into the dining room. All the kids immediately started clapping and yelling. "Yay! Way to go, Wanda! You got Magnificent Mandrake. He's the best!"

As much as I hate to admit it, Robert's show really is good. Patti, Stephanie, and I watched it through the half-open kitchen door. It was clear Robert knew his stuff. He did the vanishing quarter trick, conjured a Coke out of a section of rolled-up newspaper, poured water out of an empty glass, all leading up to the grand finale, when he announced he would pull a live hamster out of his hat.

That was when we spotted Jenny Carlin! She and Angela had sneaked through the far door, the one leading from the Kemps' living room to the dining room. And they were edging along the wall toward Mandrake!

Mandrake showed the kids his empty hat. Then he set it down on a side table, passed his hands over it, and said a few magic words. He picked it up again, reached into it, and pulled out a fat, wriggly, orange-and-white hamster!

He handed the hamster to Wanda Kemp, and

all the little kids went wild! They never cheer Sparkly and Barkly like that. Then Jenny Carlin made her move. She shot around the big round table straight toward Mandrake!

"Run for it!" Kate called to him from her place in the corner. Her video camera was still going.

Mandrake stumbled backward toward the three of us, and raced out of the dining room into the kitchen.

"You're on," Mrs. Kemp said brightly to Patti and me as Mandrake/Robert dashed for the back door. A second later, Jenny came running into the kitchen after him.

"Grab her!" Stephanie hissed.

Patti grabbed one of her wrists, and I grabbed the other. Jenny struggled, but, fortunately, she's small — Patti and I are *giants* by comparison. Pretending it was all part of our act, Sparkly and Barkly skipped cheerfully into the Kemps' dining room, pulling Jenny along between us.

"How do you keep a skunk from smelling?" Sparkly asked in her high, squeaky voice.

"Hold his nose!" Barkly growled. "Arf, arf, arf!"

Everyone burst out laughing — with the exception of Jenny Carlin, that is. Jenny glared up at us.

She looked as if she'd like to kill us both!

We told a few more jokes. Then we figured Mandrake had had enough time to make his escape, so we turned Jenny loose.

"I'll get you for this," she raged. Then she clumped upstairs with Angela behind her. As far as Jenny Carlin was concerned, the party hadn't been a success at all.

But the new, improved Sleepover Friends Party Service *was* a huge success. Mandrake was the major crowd-pleaser, of course, but the kids really liked Sparkly and Barkly, too. The new jokes we'd come up with had gone over well. And Stephanie felt great because the kids loved her caricatures. She even drew one of Wanda that made her look kind of like her new hamster. Wanda was thrilled.

When the party guests started playing musical chairs, Patti and I cleaned off our makeup. Meanwhile Kate handed Mrs. Kemp the videotape. "I think I got some great shots of Wanda — and Angela and Jenny, too," Kate told her. Then Mrs. Kemp gave us our money — forty dollars!

Still, I wasn't really surprised when on our way out Patti murmured, "I know *I* thought of it, but it doesn't seem right somehow."

98

"Making Robert join our business?" Kate asked as we walked down the front steps. "I guess I have to agree with you." She sighed. "His act is awfully good. It just doesn't seem fair taking advantage of his work so that people will hire us, too."

We got on our bikes and pedaled down the driveway onto Tuckahoe Road. "We can get business on our own," Stephanie said. "I guess. . . ."

"We'll call him from Patti's house tonight," Kate said. We were having our sleepover at the Jenkinses' that Friday.

So we were totally surprised when we found Robert Ellwanger waiting for *us* at the corner of Tuckahoe Road and Hillcrest. He and Brownie — Robert was only three years old when he named the dog, which makes it a little less nerdy — were standing on the sidewalk next to Robert's bike.

"Listen, Robert, we've been thinking it over," Kate began as we rolled up beside him.

"Right. And we've decided we're going to stop holding you up," I put in. "You're so good you deserve to be on your own."

"What we mean is, you can go back to having your own private business," Stephanie told him. She handed him fourteen dollars, easily a third of the money Mrs. Kemp had given us.

"Magnificent Mandrake and nobody else," Patti finished with a smile.

Robert Ellwanger looked sheepish. "No way," he said.

"No way?" the four of us repeated. What was that supposed to mean?

"If it hadn't been for you guys, Mandrake would have been a goner," Robert said. "Jenny Carlin would have uncovered me, and my secret, for sure. Thanks, but no thanks for your offer. There's safety in numbers!"

Patti coughed. "Robert," she said, "I think if we're going to keep being in business together it's only fair we rename ourselves Magnificent Mandrake and the Sleepover Friends Party Service." She glanced at Kate, Stephanie, and me. "Right?" she asked us.

"Right!" we all agreed.

Patti looked at Robert. "You know," she said. "You're no geek. You're really talented."

Kate, Stephanie, and I all nodded in agreement.

Robert smiled. Then he climbed on his bike. "I'll let you know if we get any calls," he said over his shoulder. Then he rode away, with Brownie gal-lumphing after him.

"Well . . . ," Kate said. She really looked sur-prised. "I guess we're still in business."

"Safety in numbers," Patti said thoughtfully. "That would make a good motto for us, don't you think?"

"I can just see it on our business cards. On one side 'Safety in numbers,' and in the middle, 'Mag-nificent Mandrake and the Sleepover Friends Party Service . . . ,' I said. "It sounds kind of great."

"And maybe at the bottom we could put, 'Sleep-over Friends forever!' " Stephanie added with a smile.

#19 The Great Kate

"What's going on?" It was Donald.

"Just what I needed!" I muttered to myself.

"Hide and seek?" Donald drawled through the window. He likes to think of himself as years older than Kate, Stephanie, Patti, and me and tons more sophisticated.

I switched off my flashlight. "No," I said. "I've lost something."

"Your mittens," Donald said. I guess he was referring to the nursery rhyme, which I didn't think was very funny at all.

"No!" I snapped. "A valuable rhinestone pin!"

Donald stared at me. "Excu-u-se me!" he huffed, slamming the window shut.

I went back to my house and quickly dialed Stephanie's private number.

She answered on the first ring. "Find it?" she asked breathlessly.

"Nope," I said.

"Oh, wow." Stephanie sounded worried. "I hope *Kate* doesn't find it. . . ."

"If she does, we'll know soon enough," I said gloomily.

WIN FIVE NIGHTSHIRTS FOR YOUR NEXT SLEEPOVER!

SLEEPOVER
FRIENDS

Enter the
SLEEPOVER FRIENDS
Super Summer Giveaway

200 Winners!

"What's your favorite thing to do at a sleepover party?"

Make your next sleepover the best ever with FIVE fabulous, oversized Sleepover Friends nightshirts for you and four friends. It's easy to win! Just tell us what's *your* favorite thing to do at a sleepover party—like telling spooky ghost stories, or doing super makeovers! Then all you have to do to enter the Sleepover Friends Super Summer Giveaway is complete the coupon below and return by November 30, 1989.

Rules: Entries must be postmarked by November 30, 1989. Winners will be picked at random from all eligible entries received. No purchase necessary. Valid only in the U.S.A. Employees of Scholastic Inc., affiliates, subsidiaries, and their families are not eligible. Void where prohibited. Winners will be notified by mail.

Fill in the coupon below or write the information on a 3″ x 5″ piece of paper and mail to: SLEEPOVER FRIENDS SUPER SUMMER GIVEAWAY, Scholastic Inc., P.O. Box 665, Cooper Station, New York, NY 10276.

Sleepover Friends Super Summer Giveaway

What's your favorite thing to do at a sleepover party?

Check one:
- ☐ Eating
- ☐ Makeovers
- ☐ Cooking
- ☐ Truth or Dare
- ☐ Telling Ghost Stories
- ☐ Other _____

Name _____ Age _____

Street _____

City, State, Zip _____

Where did you buy this *Sleepover Friends* book?
- ☐ Bookstore
- ☐ Book Fair
- ☐ Drug Store
- ☐ Book Club
- ☐ Supermarket
- ☐ Discount Store
- ☐ Other _____

SLE289

Pack your bags for fun and adventure with

SLEEPOVER FRIENDS™
by Susan Saunders

Join Kate, Lauren, Stephanie and Patti at their great sleepover parties every weekend. Truth or Dare, scary movies, late-night boy talk–it's all part of **Sleepover Friends!**

☐ MF40641-8	**#1 Patti's Luck**	**$2.50**
☐ MF40642-6	**#2 Starring Stephanie**	**$2.50**
☐ MF40643-4	**#3 Kate's Surprise**	**$2.50**
☐ MF40644-2	**#4 Patti's New Look**	**$2.50**
☐ MF41336-8	**#5 Lauren's Big Mix-Up**	**$2.50**
☐ MF41337-6	**#6 Kate's Camp-Out**	**$2.50**
☐ MF41694-4	**#7 Stephanie Strikes Back**	**$2.50**
☐ MF41695-2	**#8 Lauren's Treasure**	**$2.50**
☐ MF41696-0	**#9 No More Sleepovers, Patti?**	**$2.50**
☐ MF41697-9	**#10 Lauren's Sleepover Exchange**	**$2.50**
☐ MF41845-9	**#11 Stephanie's Family Secret**	**$2.50**
☐ MF41846-7	**#12 Kate's Sleepover Disaster**	**$2.50**
☐ MF42301-0	**#13 Patti's Secret Wish**	**$2.50**
☐ MF42300-2	**#14 Lauren Takes Charge**	**$2.50**
☐ MF42299-5	**#15 Stephanie's Big Story**	**$2.50**
☐ MF42662-1	**Sleepover Friends' Super Guide**	**$2.50**
☐ MF42366-5	**#16 Kate's Crush**	**$2.50**
☐ MF42367-3	**#17 Patti Gets Even**	**$2.50**

Available wherever you buy books...or use the coupon below.

Scholastic Inc. P.O. Box 7502, 2932 E. McCarty Street, Jefferson City, MO 65102

Please send me the books I have checked above. I am enclosing $_____

(Please add $1.00 to cover shipping and handling). Send check or money order–no cash or C.O.D.'s please

Name _____

Address _____

City _____ State/Zip _____

Please allow four to six weeks for delivery. Offer good in U.S.A. only. Sorry, mail order not available to residents of Canada. Prices subject to change.

SLE 289